COCK-A-DOODLE-DOO

WHEN · THE · ROOSTER · CROWED ·

by Patricia Lillie

pictures by

Nancy Winslow Parker

HARCOURT BRACE & COMPANY

Orlando   Atlanta   Austin   Boston   San Francisco   Chicago   Dallas   New York
Toronto   London

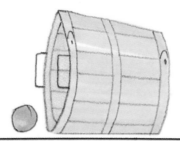

This edition is published by special arrangement with William Morrow
& Company, Inc. Grateful acknowledgment is made to William Morrow
& Company, Inc. for permission to reprint *When the Rooster Crowed* by
Patricia Lillie, illustrated by Nancy Winslow Parker. Text copyright © 1991
by Patricia Lillie; illustrations copyright © 1991 by Nancy Winslow Parker.

Printed in the United States of America
ISBN 0-15-301471-7
9   10   035   97   96

FOR MOM AND DAD
—P. L.

FOR SELMA LANES
—N. W. P.

When the sun came over the hill,
the rooster crowed, "Cock-a-doodle-doo!"

"Ten more minutes,"
said the farmer.

When the cow said, "Mmmooo,"
the rooster crowed, "Cock-a-doodle-doo!"

"Five more minutes,"
said the farmer.

When the horse went, "Neigh,"
the rooster crowed, "Cock-a-doodle-doo!"

"Just a few more minutes,"
said the farmer.

When the pigs went, "Oink, Oink,"
the rooster crowed, "Cock-a-doodle-doo!"

"One more minute,"
said the farmer.

When the chickens said, "Cluck, Cluck, Cluck,"
the rooster crowed, "Cock-a-doodle-doo!"

"Half a minute,"
said the farmer.

When the farmer's wife yelled, "ALBERT!"
the rooster crowed, "Cock-a-doodle-doo!"

"In a second,"
said the farmer.

But when the cow said,
"MMMOOO,"

and the horse said,
"NEIGH!"

and the pigs said,
"OINK, OINK,"

and the chickens said,
"CLUCK, CLUCK, CLUCK,"

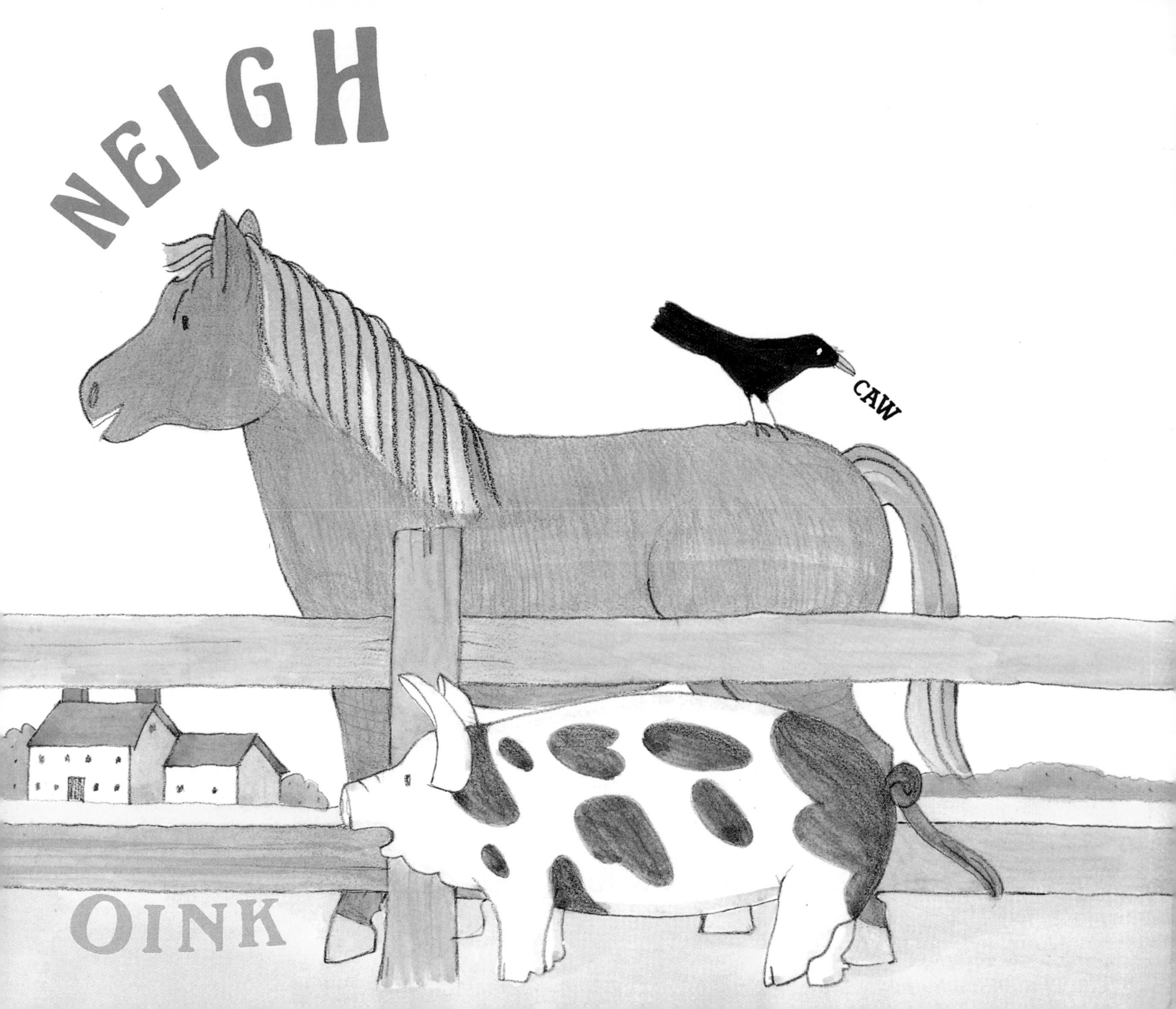
NEIGH
CAW
OINK

and the farmer's wife yelled, "ALBERT!"

and the rooster crowed,
"COCK-A-DOODLE-DOO!"
all at the same time . . .

COCK-A-DOODLE-DOO

the farmer said, "ALL RIGHT!"

He jumped out of bed,

pulled on his clothes,

milked the cow,

fed the horse,

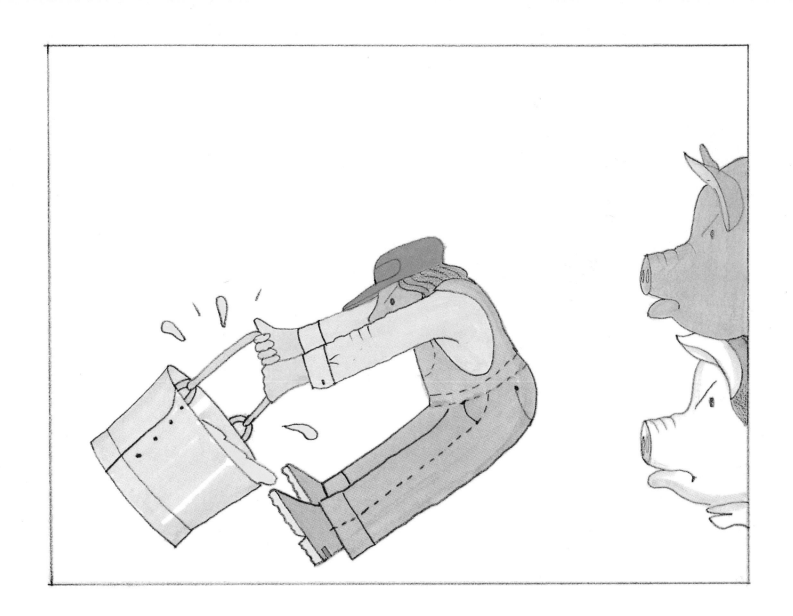

slopped the pigs,

gathered the eggs,

and

sat down for breakfast.